CIRCLE

by

Mac Barnett

&

Jon Klassen

WALKER BOOKS
AND SUBSIDIARIES
LONDON · BOSTON · SYDNEY · AUCKLAND

ROYAL BOROUGH OF GREENWICH

Follow us on twitter @greenwichlibs

Please return by the last date shown

04/21	- 2 NOV 2021	
1 5 MAY 2021	3 1 DEC 2021	2 4 DEC 2022
- 9 JUN 2022	7 APR 2022	2 6 MAY 2024
- 8 JUL 2021	2 8 JUL 2023	
2 8 AUG 2021		
2 3 MAR 2022	2 4 NOV 2023	

Thank you! To renew, please contact any
Royal Greenwich library or renew online or by phone
www.better.org.uk/greenwichlibraries
24hr renewal line 01527 852385

First published

2019 by Walker Books Ltd, 87 Vauxhall

Walk, London SE11 5HJ • This edition published

2020 • Text © 2019 Mac Barnett • Illustrations © 2019

Jon Klassen • The moral rights of the author and illustrator

have been asserted • This book has been typeset in New Century

Schoolbook • Printed in China • All rights reserved. No part of this

book may be reproduced, transmitted or stored in an information

retrieval system in any form or by any means, graphic, electronic or

mechanical, including photocopying, taping and recording, without

prior written permission from the publisher. • British Library

Cataloguing in Publication Data: a catalogue record for

this book is available from the British Library

ISBN 978-1-4063-9037-7 • www.walker.co.uk

2 4 6 8 10 9 7 5 3

This is Circle.

This is Circle's waterfall.

One day, Circle and Square and Triangle
played a game near her waterfall.
"Here are the rules," Circle said.
"I will close my eyes and count to ten.
You must hide somewhere.
When I open my eyes, I will try to find you."
Square said, "OK."
Triangle said, "Neat!"

"There is one more rule," said Circle.
"No hiding behind the waterfall."
Square said, "OK."
Triangle said, "Why not?"
"Because," said Circle. "It is dark back there."
Square said, "OK."
Triangle said, "I am not afraid of the dark!"

Circle closed her eyes and counted to ten.
"Ready or not," said Circle, "here I come!"

When she opened her eyes,
Square was just standing there.
He pointed and said,
"Triangle went behind the waterfall."

Circle sighed. "I will go find him."

"Circle," said Square, "you are very brave."

"I know," Circle said.

And she slipped behind the waterfall.

It was quiet on the other side of the waterfall.
Circle called out, "Triangle! Triangle! Where are you?"

There was no answer.

Farther inside, there was not much light.

"Triangle! Triangle! Where are you!"

There was no answer. She went even farther

until it was all dark.

"Triangle!" said Circle. "There you are!
Why do you always break all the rules?"
There was no answer.

"Why do you always spoil our fun?"
There was no answer.
"Why are you such a bad friend?"
There was no answer.

"I'm sorry," said Circle.

"I should not have said that.

You are a good friend.

You just made us worried.

We love you, Triangle."

"Thanks!" Triangle said from behind her.
Circle turned around and said, "Triangle?"
"Yes!" said Triangle. "I am sure glad to see
you and Square!"

Circle said, "Square is outside.

This is not Square. I thought it was you."

"No," said Triangle, "that is not me."

"No," said Circle.

"Oh," said Triangle.

Circle turned back and faced the shape in the dark.
"Who are you?" she asked.

There was no answer.

"AAAH!" said Triangle.

Triangle and Circle ran very fast, back through the dark.

Back through where there was not much light.

Back through the waterfall, back to the outside.

Square was waiting there for them.
They told him what had happened.
"Well," Square said, "I am glad I stayed here!"
Triangle said, "Now I am afraid of the dark!"
Circle looked back at the waterfall falling.
"You know," she said, "that shape in the dark might
not have been bad. It might have been a good shape.
We just could not see it."

Circle closed her eyes.

"I wonder," Circle said. "What kind of shape was it?"

Then they all closed their eyes,

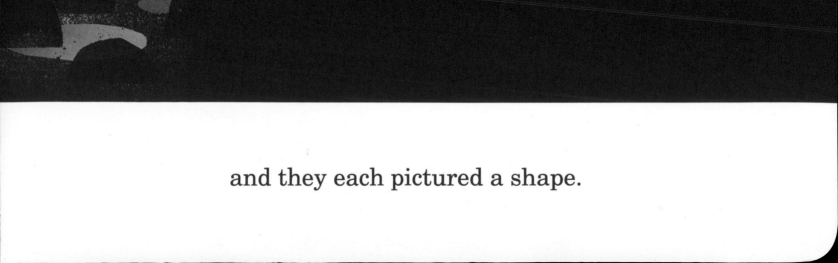

and they each pictured a shape.

If you close your eyes, what shape do you picture?

To the Villalongs:
Dan, Katherine, Elsa, Margot, and Helena

M. B.

For Ann Stott, with thanks for all you do

J. K.

MAC BARNETT & JON KLASSEN
have made six books together: *Sam and Dave Dig a Hole, Extra Yarn, The Wolf, the Duck and the Mouse, Triangle, Square* and *Circle,* which is the book you are reading right now. Jon is also the creator of the much-acclaimed Hat trilogy, which includes *I Want My Hat Back,* the Kate Greenaway and Caldecott Medal winner *This Is Not My Hat* and *We Found a Hat*. They both live in California, USA, but in different cities. Jon's Canadian; Mac's not.